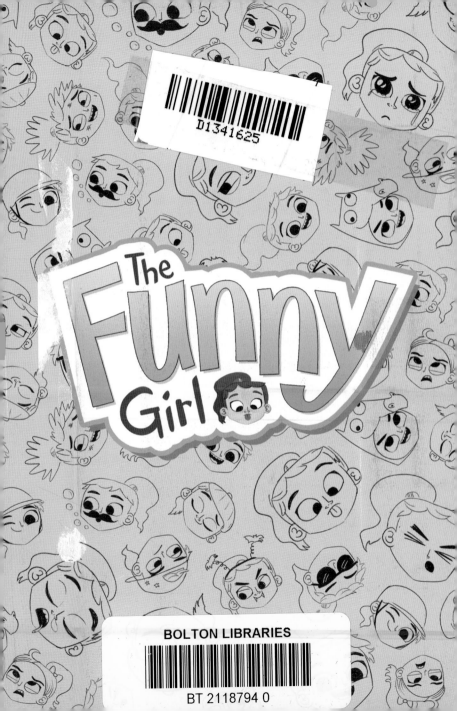

The Funny Girl

Raintree is an imprint of Capstone Global Library Limited, a company
incorporated in England and Wales having its registered office at 264 Banbury
Road, Oxford, OX2 7DY – Registered company number: 6695582

www.raintree.co.uk
myorders@raintree.co.uk

Designed by Hilary Wacholz
Original illustrations © Capstone Global Library Limited 2019
Originated by Capstone Global Library Ltd
Printed and bound in India

ISBN 978 1 4747 6197 0
22 21 20 19 18
10 9 8 7 6 5 4 3 2 1

British Library Cataloguing in Publication Data
A full catalogue record for this book is available from the British Library.

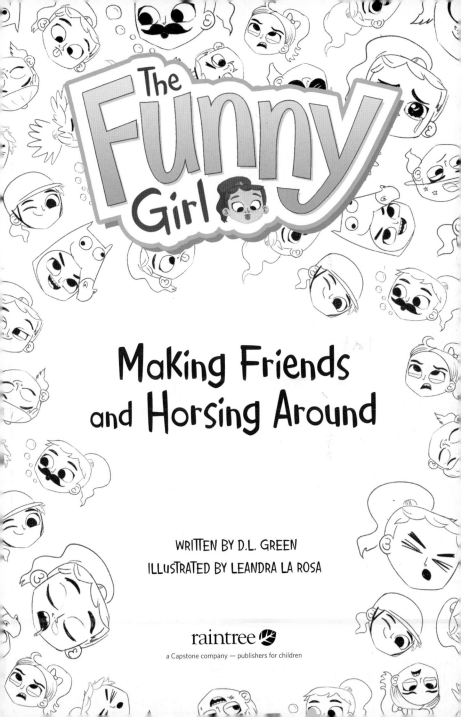

The Funny Girl

Making Friends and Horsing Around

WRITTEN BY D.L. GREEN

ILLUSTRATED BY LEANDRA LA ROSA

raintree

a Capstone company — publishers for children

CONTENTS

A HUGE TINY PROBLEM

The trip from Ohio to Los Angeles took a thousand days. Actually, four days. But it felt like a thousand. There was nothing worse than being stuck in the car with my family. At least the long ride was almost over.

I pointed to a pink Toyota in front of us and said, "If everyone had cars like that, we'd be a pink car nation."

Dad laughed. "Pink carnation. Good one, Shelby!"

Mum said, "I should post that joke on my blog."

My mum puts stuff on her blog about a thousand times a day. Already today she had posted pictures of:

A sign that said, "Welcome to California".

Graffiti under the sign that said, "Now get out".

A cockroach in a petrol station toilet.

Me, asleep in the car with drool on my chin.

I looked at the pictures on Mum's phone while I sat in the back seat of the car. When I saw the picture of me sleeping and drooling, I told Mum, "I wish you hadn't posted that on your blog."

"But you look so sweet in the picture, like a baby," Mum said.

"I look like I have drool on my chin," I replied.

"Yes, like a baby. Babies drool a lot," Mum said. "Your picture got eight hundred likes."

"The cockroach in the petrol station toilet got two thousand likes!" I complained.

Mum smiled. "My blog is really getting popular."

I rolled my eyes.

Mum took a picture of me rolling my eyes.

I hoped no one at my new school read Mum's blog. No one would want to be friends with a drooling baby. What if the kids at my new school gave me a mean nickname like Drooly or Rolly-Eye?

"Cheer up, Shelby," my dad said. Then he started singing: "It's a road trip! Not a toad trip! Or a road drip! So smile, smile, smile!"

I did not smile, smile, smile. I did not even smile.

"That song might work for my show," Dad said. He was starting a new job in Los Angeles. That's why we were moving. He was going to write for a children's TV programme called *Everyone Loves a Clown*.

Not everyone loves a clown. I do not love clowns. I don't even like them much. I love my dad, though.

"Smile, smile, smile!" my little brother, Coop, shouted. He was four years old. I didn't know if all four-year-olds shouted a lot, but Coop certainly did.

"Coop, please keep your voice down," my older sister, Miss Priss, said. Her real name is Lila, but I call her Miss Priss sometimes because she is very prissy. Lila and I are close in age – only a year apart – but not at all close in personality. For instance, Lila is always brushing and styling her long hair. She keeps her clothes neatly folded in her chest of drawers.

Not me. I usually shove my hair in a sloppy ponytail and toss my clothes on the floor of my wardrobe.

The only member of our family keeping quiet in that car was our dog, Mugsy. He's a mutt. If you took the biggest, hairiest dogs you ever saw and mixed them together, you'd have Mugsy. He's huge, and he sheds a lot. I mean a *lot*. He's like that King Midas guy who made everything he touched turn into gold. Except Mugsy turns everything he touches into hair. Also, Mugsy is clumsy and not very bright. Also, he's the best dog in the universe.

"We're almost at our new house!" Mum said.

I looked out of the window. We passed little bungalows

with small front gardens and hardly any space between them.

"Is this our street?" Lila asked.

"No," Mum said.

Good. Those houses were small.

Dad turned and drove down a street with even smaller houses. Their front gardens were smaller too – more like tiny patches of grass than gardens. Some houses didn't have grass at all – just cactuses or small rocks.

Dad turned into the driveway of a tiny white house and said, "We've made it!"

I looked out of the car window. Yellow-green grass covered the lawn. **If the grass could talk, it would say in a hoarse voice, "Water me."** The house was shaped like a small rectangle. **If the house could talk, it would have a tiny voice and say, "I'm tiny."**

"I don't mean to complain," Lila said. "But this house looks tiny."

"That was a complaint," I said.

"Where's the rest of the house?" Coop asked.

"Why didn't you tell us we were moving into a doll's house?" I asked.

"It's not a doll's house," Mum said as she got out of the car.

"We didn't want you to worry," Dad said as he got out too.

I stayed in the car and crossed my arms. "Let's just go back to Ohio."

Dad laughed, even though I wasn't joking.

Mum slid open the door of the car, leaned in and aimed her camera at me. "Smile!" she said.

I still did not smile.

I finally got out of the car and walked through our new house. It didn't take long. The front garden was small. Every room inside was small. The back garden was small.

In a small voice, Lila said, "I only saw three bedrooms."

"We didn't want you to worry," Dad repeated. "You'll be sharing a bedroom."

Lila frowned and pointed to me. "With her?"

I frowned and pointed to Lila. "With her?"

Mum and Dad nodded.

"You'd better not be messy," Lila said.

"You'd better not be prissy," I said. "Too late. You already are."

"Stop that, Shelby," Dad said.

While my parents weren't looking, Lila stuck out her tongue at me.

I stuck out my tongue back at her.

That time my parents *were* looking. In fact, Mum took a picture of me with my tongue out.

Dad frowned and said, "Shelby Bloom! Go to your room!"

It turns out there was something worse than being stuck with my family in a car – being stuck with my family in a tiny house in a strange city.

2

PHEW, PHEW, PHEW, PHEW, UH-OH

Right after Dad said, "Shelby Bloom! Go to your room!" he said, "Hey, that rhymes: Shelby Bloom. Go to your room." He started singing, "Shelby Bloom went to her room! Zoom, zoom, zoom! She rode a broom!"

"Rode a broom? Are you saying I'm a witch?" I asked.

"No," Dad said. "I was just thinking of a rhyme for *Bloom*."

"How about *doom*? Or *gloom*?" I said, trying to make him forget about sending me to my room.

"*Doom* and *gloom*?" Dad asked. "Aren't there any happier rhymes for *Bloom*?"

"Tomb," I said.

Dad laughed. His head shook, looking kind of like a fuzzy ping-pong ball.

I tried to distract him again. I said, "You shouldn't have named me Shelby. Nothing rhymes with *Shelby*."

Dad nodded. "I should have named you Grace. There are so many rhymes for *Grace* – race, lace, face. Or I could have named you Kate – late, fate, wait."

My distraction plan had worked.

"Dad, don't forget you sent Shelby to her room," Lila said.

I glared at her.

"I am just trying to help," Lila said in her prissiest voice.

"Can I take a closer look at the front garden?" I asked. Before Dad had a chance to answer, I hurried outside.

I heard loud thumps across the street. A boy about my age was dribbling a basketball in his driveway. He threw the ball towards the hoop in front of his garage. His shot banged off the backboard and rolled back to him.

I took a deep breath and walked over.

I said, "Hey, did you know babies are good at basketball? They're always dribbling."

The boy laughed.

Phew!

"You know who's not good at basketball? Cinderella," I said. "She ran away from the ball."

He laughed again.

Double phew!

"I'm Shelby Bloom." I pointed to my new house. "My family just moved here."

"Great. I'm Ajay Patel." He swiped a strand of hair off his forehead. "My family has been here since before I was born. Do you shoot hoops?"

"Only if they try to shoot me first."

Ajay laughed again.

Triple phew!

I stole the ball from him and took a shot. The ball landed about a thousand miles from the hoop. I was much better at jokes than I was at basketball.

Ajay chased down the ball and took a shot. He missed the hoop by about a thousand miles too.

"I guess we're not exactly ready for the NBA," he said.

"Unless the NBA stands for No Basketball Ability," I said.

He laughed again. "You're funny!"

"Thanks," I said.

I hadn't smiled when Mum and Dad asked me to earlier, but I was smiling now. I had made a friend so fast!

We played basketball. We each took about a thousand more shots and each only got one in the basket. It was sunny outside and much less humid than it was in Ohio. Plus there were no mosquitos to worry about. California had its good points.

Finally, I held the ball and leaned against Ajay's garage

door. I said, "Do you go to Grimwood School?"

Ajay nodded. "I'm starting back there in two days."

Quadruple phew! "Me too. Is Grimwood grim?"

"Not really. Grimwood is an OK school. I've been going there for years. So have most of the kids," Ajay said. "I've had the same group of friends since I was five years old. All boys, of course."

"Oh." I gulped. "Do you ever let new people join your group of friends?"

"Not really." Ajay shrugged. "We don't get many new people at our school."

"Do you ever let girls join your group?" I asked.

Ajay shook his head.

So Ajay wasn't my friend after all. I wondered if anyone would let me into their friend group. The basketball slipped through my fingers and rolled down the driveway. It landed in the gutter. Kind of like my life.

THOUSANDS OF WRONG THINGS

"Get off me!" I shouted. Thousands of bees were chasing me and buzzing loudly. They buzzed past my ears again and again.

I sat up in bed and opened my eyes.

Oh. The bees were only in my nightmare. My sister's alarm clock was buzzing loudly again and again.

"Turn that thing off!" I yelled.

She did.

I rubbed my eyes and looked at Lila's clock.

"Ack!" I said. The alarm clock was even scarier than thousands of bees.

"What's wrong?" Lila asked.

"Three things are wrong. For one thing, your alarm clock has a picture of Dalton Dash on it."

"That's not wrong. That's totally right." Lila bent down and kissed the big sticker of Dalton Dash's face that she had plastered on her clock. She kissed it right on the lips.

"Yuck!" I said.

"Yum!" she said. "Dalton Dash is the sweetest, cutest, best singer ever."

I shook my head. "The second wrong thing is that it's 5:45 in the morning."

"I like to wake up early," Lila said. "I like to see the sunrise and have plenty of time to get ready for school."

"I like to wake up late, miss the sunrise and get ready for school fast," I said.

"We're walking to the bus stop together," Lila said. "You'd better not make me late."

"I'm going back to sleep," I said.

"Wait. What's the third wrong thing?" Lila asked.

"The third wrong thing is that I have to share a room with you." I pulled my duvet over my face and closed my eyes.

I didn't sleep for long. I had a nightmare that someone was throwing vomit and dog poo in my face. I sat up in my bed and opened my eyes again. Oh. It wasn't a nightmare. Lila had thrown vomit and dog poo in my face.

"Be careful with that," I said. "It's very precious to me."

"Keep your fake throw-up and poo on your side of the drawers," Lila said.

I got out of bed and put the rubber vomit and plastic dog poo on my side of the drawers. Then I took a large fake insect from one of the drawers and put it in my backpack. One of my life mottoes was: You never know when you'll need a large fake insect.

"You need to hurry and get ready," Lila said. "We have to leave for school soon."

"No problem," I said.

Except it was a problem. It took me about a thousand hours to get dressed. I hadn't unpacked my clothes yet, so I had to search for them in the moving boxes on my side of the room. Lila's side was neat and tidy, of course.

Plus I didn't know what clothes would fit in with the kids at my new school. On TV, people who lived in California mostly wore sunglasses and bathing suits. I didn't think they dressed like that for school, but I wasn't completely sure.

I finally just put on jeans and a brown T-shirt that was a little wrinkled. I went into the kitchen.

Lila was there, wearing a bright white dress and already washing her dishes. "Thank you for making a healthy breakfast," she told Dad.

I rolled my eyes at Miss Priss.

Mum snapped a picture of me.

Then I wolfed down some eggs. Mum took a picture of that too.

My first day of school was off to a bad start. And evidence of that bad start would soon be posted on Mum's blog.

THE WORST WRONG THING OF ALL

On the first day of school, my whole family walked to the bus stop together.

Well, Coop didn't walk. He ran in circles around us and shouted, "I'm underpants spinning in a dryer!" Every so often, he fell on his bottom. But he kept getting up and spinning again.

Mum recorded a video of him. She said, "This will look so cute on my blog!"

"I just thought of a fantastic rhyme for *bus stop: rust top*," Dad said. Then he sang, "The rust top on the bus stop! It is a must stop!"

"Can Lila and I walk to the bus stop by ourselves from now on?" I asked.

"Why?" Mum asked.

Coop shouted, "Underpants! Underpants! Underpants!"

"That is one reason why," Lila said.

Dad sang, "The rust top on the bus stop! It's a must stop! For clowns! And hounds! And people all around!"

"And that is another reason," I said.

"Everyone smile for more pictures," Mum said.

"That's a third reason why we want to walk by ourselves," Lila said.

At least Lila and I agreed on something.

Ajay and some other kids were waiting at the bus stop.

No one was wearing bathing suits, and only one girl wore sunglasses. Some of the girls wore dresses like Lila, but some wore T-shirts and jeans like me. I hoped some of the kids would be my friends.

"We can stay here with you until the bus comes," my dad said.

"No, thank you," Lila said.

"Please don't," I added.

Mum and Dad gave us quick kisses. Coop gave us big hugs. Then they left.

I walked over to Ajay, who was talking to another boy. I joked, "I bet you can't wait to sit in a classroom all day and start doing homework again."

Ajay laughed. But the boy next to him frowned and said, "Girls are so weird."

"It was a joke," I said. "Like this one: Why didn't anyone take the bus to school?"

Ajay and the other boy glanced at each other.

"Because the bus wouldn't fit through the school door," I said.

Ajay smiled.

The other boy said, "Why would anyone try to put a bus through a door? That's weird."

Ajay's smile disappeared. He said, "Yeah, that's weird."

My face flushed with anger. I glared at Ajay and walked away.

I heard a girl tell Lila that she liked her dress. Another girl said Lila had pretty hair.

I went over to three girls who looked about my age. They were huddled close together. They didn't open the huddle to me.

One of the girls looked at me and said, "Hi."

I gave her a big friendly smile and said, "Hi! I'm Shelby Bloom."

She pointed to my feet. "Your shoes don't match."

I looked down. Oh no! I was wearing my old grey trainer on one foot and my new blue trainer on the other foot. In my rush to get ready, I hadn't noticed.

The girls in the huddle looked at my feet and laughed.

There was no way I could go to a new school like this. I would die of embarrassment. I'd have to run home and change. If I hurried, I could put on the right shoes before the bus came.

Then the bus pulled up.

WHAT'S THE FRENCH WORD FOR *FRIEND?*

I had a seat to myself on the school bus. That was fine by me. Maybe I could work out what to do about my mismatched shoes.

No one would distract me.

Except the girls sitting across the aisle from me. They pointed at my shoes and whispered to each other. But no one else could distract me.

Except Ajay and his friend, who sat in front of me talking about their favourite basketball players. But no one else could distract me.

Except Lila and a girl named Lola. I heard them sit behind me and tell each other their names. Lila said she liked Lola's backpack. Lola said she liked Lila's dress. Lila said she liked Lola's hairstyle. Lola said she liked Lila's shoes.

I looked down at my shoes. No one liked mismatched shoes. No one would like a girl who wore mismatched shoes.

Quickly I thought of three excuses for wearing them:

1. Our house had burned down. I had only been able to save my dog, my little brother and these two mismatched shoes.

2. I had donated my other shoes to two one-footed children. One child wanted my grey trainer. The other wanted my blue trainer.

3. A gang of shoe thieves had stolen all my shoes except the two I was wearing.

None of those excuses sounded good. I decided to stay on the bus until school ended and I could ride back home. I would start school tomorrow wearing matching shoes.

I stayed in my seat while the other kids got off the bus.

"This is your school, isn't it?" the bus driver asked me.

I nodded.

"So get off my bus and go to class."

I sighed and got off the bus.

I walked to my new classroom. Ajay and two other boys stood outside the closed door. A skinny girl with wavy black hair sat cross-legged on the floor, reading a book. Two other girls stood next to each other, whispering.

One of the girls stopped whispering and stared at me. She was about my height and wore a purple dress, a red jumper, metal bracelets on her wrist and a fake flower in her hair. She said, "You're new to the school."

I nodded.

The girl pointed at my shoes.

I opened my mouth to tell her that these shoes were the only ones saved from a big fire.

But before I could talk, the girl said, "Are mismatched shoes a thing where you used to live?"

That sounded a lot better than the excuses I had come up with. So I said, "Yes. Mismatched shoes are super stylish where I used to live."

"That is so cool!" the girl said.

"It is?" I asked. Then I said, "I mean, it is. Mismatched shoes are very cool in some places."

"I'm Brooke," the girl said.

"I'm Shelby," I said.

"I'm Tessa. We love fashion," the girl next to Brooke said. Tessa was the same height as Brooke and dressed like her. She wore a striped grey dress with a green belt. She also had a fake flower in her hair.

"I like your fashion-forward style." Brooke looked at my shoes again.

"I call it my soleful style," I joked. "Full of S-O-L-E sole. Get it?"

Brooke and Tessa did not laugh.

But the girl sitting on the floor laughed. She looked up from her book and said, "Brooke would walk a mile in your shoes."

I giggled.

Brooke did not giggle. She did not even smile. She said, "Where are you from, Shelby?"

"Bunktown, Ohio," I said.

Brooke frowned. "I've never heard of Bunktown, Ohio."

"Me neither," Tessa said.

"You must not be fashion forward after all," Brooke said before she turned away from me.

Oh no! I had to do something. I said, "Last year I lived in a very fashion-forward city."

Brooke ignored me.

But the girl with the book said, "What city?"

"Um . . . um . . . Paris," I said.

Brooke turned around. "Paris, France?"

I nodded. "They call it the fashion-forward capital of the world."

"Ooh!" Brooke said.

"We love fashion," Tessa said.

"What's Paris like?" Brooke asked.

"It's very French," I said.

"Tell me more," Brooke said.

"It has, um, the Eiffel Tower, which is, um, really tall."

Brooke crossed her arms.

I added, "All the restaurants have French fries. Great French fries. Very tasty French fries."

"But what about French fashion?" Brooke asked.

"We love fashion," Tessa said again.

"In France, mismatched shoes are very hot," I said.

"We'll all wear mismatched shoes tomorrow," Brooke said.

"Ooh! So fashion forward!" Tessa said.

"Sit with us at lunch today," Brooke said.

"OK!" I had made new friends!

Just then a plump woman with greying hair opened the classroom door, smiled widely and said, "Welcome, everyone!"

The kids around me said "Good morning" or "Hello, Ms Fish."

We all walked into the classroom.

Brooke turned to me and said, "During lunch, you can tell us all about French fashion."

"I can?" I gulped. "I mean, I can."

I had already said all I knew about French fashion – nothing. What else could I say about it at lunchtime? A whole lot of nothing.

I didn't even know the French word for *nothing*.

SOMETHING'S FISHY

Brooke, Tessa and I sat at a small table near the back of the classroom.

After the bell rang and everyone was seated, the teacher said, "Hello, class. I'm Ms Fish. I've been teaching here since the school opened thirty years ago."

"Everyone knows that," Brooke whispered.

Everyone but me, I thought.

"I have taught many of your brothers and sisters," Ms Fish said.

Not mine.

A boy put up his hand. "You were my dad's teacher."

"Terrific! Your dad is Little Larry, right?" Ms Fish said.

"Now they call him Big Larry," the boy said.

"Good," Ms Fish said. "Now let's go around the room and say our names so we can all meet each other."

A girl put up her hand. "We already know each other from last year."

"And the year before," Ajay said.

"And the years before that," a boy said.

"Not everyone was here last year," Ms Fish said.

All the kids stared at me.

Two girls pointed at my shoes and whispered.

I looked away. We took turns saying our names.

Brooke said, "I am Brooke Crumpkin. But you all know that, of course."

Tessa said, "I'm Tessa Lee. Obviously."

I thought of something: **If Tessa's parents had named her Obvious, then she would be Obvious Lee.** Then I thought of something else: **What if her whole family had adjectives for names? Careful Lee, Free Lee, Cold Lee.**

Ms Fish patted my shoulder. "And what is your name?"

I looked around. All the kids were staring at me. Some of them were laughing.

"Were you in a trance or something?" a boy said.

Oh no! While I had been thinking about names for the Lees, the class had been waiting for me to say my name.

"Sorry," I said.

"Your name is Sorry?" a boy said.

"No," I said.

"Your name is No?" he said.

"That's enough." Ms Fish gave the boy a mean stare I've seen teachers use before – the one where their eyes and lips somehow get thinner.

Then Ms Fish patted my shoulder again and said, "Tell

the class your name." She used the same soothing tone my old teacher had used after our class lost the Reading Rangers contest by two measly points and missed out on a pizza party.

Just thinking about that lost pizza party still made me upset.

"What's your name?" Ms Fish asked me for the third time.

Oh no! I had been lost in thought again.

Finally I said, "I'm Shelby Bloom."

"She just moved here from France," Brooke said.

"Wonderful!" Ms Fish said. *"Bonjour."*

Luckily, I knew that was the French word for *hello*. Even luckier, I knew how to say *thank you* in French. So I said, *"Merci."*

The teacher smiled and said something else. Something very long. Something that may have been French. Or possibly Martian. It sounded like, *"Moola malla boola balla blah blah blah?"*

"Aren't you going to answer Ms Fish's question?" Brooke said. "After spending a year in France, you must know French."

I took a deep breath. Then I made up some words: *"Zoola Zahla poola pahla blah blah blah."*

Ms Fish stopped smiling. She raised her eyebrows.

Brooke whispered, "Was that really French?"

I nodded.

"It sounded like made-up words," Brooke said.

"Welcome, Shelby Bloom," Ms Fish said in English.

We kept going around the room. The rest of the kids said their names. I found out that the girl who had been reading outside the classroom this morning was called Gabby Garcia.

"Class, I have a fun project for you," Ms Fish said. "It involves something you love."

We all grinned.

"It also involves writing," she added.

Most of us stopped grinning.

"I want each of you to write five sentences about something you love."

I thought about what to write. I loved a lot of things. I loved jokes. I loved my dog. I loved pizza. It was hard to choose just one thing to write about. If my dog delivered pizzas while telling jokes, I would definitely write about that.

"We love fashion," Tessa said.

"We will all write about fashion," Brooke said. "I love my silk scarf from Italy. I will write about my beautiful scarf."

Tessa said, "I will write about my cashmere jumper from Nepal."

I said, "I will write about my polyester socks from Ohio."

"Huh?" Brooke asked.

"I was joking," I said.

Brooke frowned. "Fashion is nothing to joke about."

"We love fashion," Tessa said.

"I know." I sighed. "OK. I'll write about my clothes from France."

"What clothes?" Brooke asked.

"Um, my hat," I said. "My fashion-forward French hat."

"You mean your beret, right?" Brooke said.

"What?" I asked.

"Beret." Brooke crossed her arms. "The French word for *hat*."

"It is?" I asked. "I mean, of course it is."

"Girls, you should be writing, not whispering to each other," Ms Fish said.

I picked up a pencil and stared at the paper in front of me. I could not think of five sentences to write about a beret. I could not think of *one* sentence to write about a beret. I did not know what kind of hat a beret was.

"Everyone should be writing," Ms Fish said.

I started writing:

I really like my French hat.
It is called a beret.

That is a French word for *hat*.

In France, a hat is called a beret.

I have written five sentences about my beret, if you include this one.

You should include it.

Now I have written seven sentences.

I should get extra credit.

Now I'm up to nine sentences.

I wrote fifteen sentences about a beret and about writing about a beret. And at the end, I still did not know what a beret looked like.

When the lunch bell rang, Brooke exclaimed, "The lunch bell is the best sound ever!"

It was not. The best sound ever was the bell at the end of the school day. Or ice cream van music.

Today the lunch bell was the worst sound ever. I had to tell my new friends about French fashion. I knew nothing about French fashion. And if Brooke and Tessa found out, they would want nothing to do with me.

FRANCE CERTAINLY SEEMS STRANGE

I sat across from Brooke and Tessa at the lunch table. Gabby Garcia sat nearby, eating a sandwich and reading a book. She was hunched over. Her long black hair covered half her face.

I had a life motto: You never know when you'll need a large fake insect.

I had other life mottoes too. For instance: When in doubt, tell a joke.

If I could make Brooke and Tessa laugh all through lunch, they might forget about French fashion. I said, "Do you know what's the worst thing in the canteen?"

Brooke shrugged.

"The food," I said.

Gabby looked up from her book and laughed.

"Huh?" Brooke asked.

"It's a joke," I said.

"Good one," Gabby said.

"Want to hear more?" I asked.

Brooke shook her head. "I want to hear about French fashion."

"We love fashion," Tessa said.

"I know," I said.

I pictured my clothes at home in the moving boxes. I also pictured my clothes I'd thrown near the moving boxes. A lot of my clothes were blue because that was my favourite colour.

So I said, "In France, the colour blue is very trendy."

"Ooh!" Tessa exclaimed.

"Everyone in France wears blue jeans," I said, because I liked wearing blue jeans.

"What kind of blue jeans?" Brooke asked.

What? The kind of jeans that were blue. What other kinds were there?

I took a big bite of my apple so I didn't have to answer Brooke's question.

"Boyfriend jeans? Mum jeans? Dad jeans? Skinny jeans? Bootcut?" Tessa asked.

"Slouch? Flared leg? Cropped? Capri? Low rise? High rise? Midrise?" Brooke asked.

"Not boyfriend jeans," I said. I did not want a boyfriend. I did not want anything to do with a boyfriend. "Not parent jeans either."

"Parent jeans?" Brooke asked.

"You mean mum jeans and dad jeans?" Tessa asked.

"Um, yeah," I said. "Who would want to wear their parents' jeans?"

"So what kind of jeans are fashion forward in France?" Brooke asked.

"Too-small jeans," I said.

Tessa leaned towards me. "Ooh! What's that?"

"Jeans that you're growing out of. Jeans that are a bit short on you." I said that because I was growing out of my jeans.

"Cool," Brooke said.

"We love fashion," Tessa said.

"I think you may have mentioned that before," I said.

Gabby Garcia giggled. Then she returned to her book.

"What else is trendy in France?" Brooke asked.

I thought of other things I had at home. "Large bracelets."

"Ooh!" Tessa said.

"The trendiest bracelet colour is white," I said, because the only bracelet I owned was white.

"What else do French people wear?" Tessa asked.

I took a long, slow drink of milk while I tried to think up other fashion-forward things.

"You'd better be telling the truth," Brooke said.

I spilled milk on my top.

"Uh-oh! Is that top from France?" Tessa asked.

I nodded. "Yes, but I can still wear it. French people don't mind when their clothes get stained. In fact, stains are very fashion forward."

"Ooh!" Tessa said.

"If you are making things up, I'll be really mad," Brooke said.

"Don't worry," I said.

"I'm not worried," Tessa said.

I wasn't worried either.

I was terrified.

ALMOST AS BAD AS A YELLOW PUDDLE

After lunch, Ms Fish explained about a thousand class rules and taught us some maths and history. I was tired by the time I got on the school bus. Still, I wished I had someone to talk to. Lila and Lola sat in front of me. They whispered and giggled together the whole way home. Ajay and his friend sat behind me and talked every so often to each other. I sat by myself again.

Today had not been the worst day ever. The worst day ever was back in first year when I'd wet myself in class. The girl sitting next to me had yelled, "Yuck! Shelby Bloom made a wee puddle!" I tried claiming it had rained on me. Even six-year-olds were too smart to believe it had rained inside the classroom and only on my trousers and chair. Nothing could be worse than that day.

Today I was wee-free. And I had convinced Brooke and Tessa that my mismatched shoes and stained top were fashion forward. Still, I didn't like to lie. Today was probably the second-worst day ever.

When I got off the bus, I saw Mum, Dad, Coop and Mugsy waiting for us. That made me feel a little better.

I patted Coop's head. Then I patted Mugsy's head. I got dog hairs all over my hand.

Mum took a video of Lila and Lola hugging goodbye.

"Let's go," I said.

We started walking home.

Coop pointed at me. "You're wearing a frowny face."

My dad started singing, "Turn that frown upside-down! Like a clown! On a playground!"

"I am in no mood for songs," I told Dad.

"Now you're wearing a grouchy face," Coop said.

"Shelby," Mum said, "you're growing out of your blue jeans. I'm taking you shopping today for new jeans."

"I don't want new jeans," I said. "I need some new French clothes."

"What?" Mum asked.

"Clothes from France. Not just France. They have to be from Paris, France. And I need a beret right away."

"Hey, that rhymes," Dad said. He sang, "A beret! Right away! Needed today! Oy vey!"

"A beret?" Mum said. "Why do you need a silly hat? Is your school having Crazy Hat Day?"

I nodded.

"I don't know which shops sell berets," Mum said. "But we have a couple of sombreros from a Cinco De Mayo party we went to. You and Lila can wear those tomorrow."

"Thank you, Mother. And thank you, Shelby. I didn't know it was Crazy Hat Day tomorrow," Lila said.

I didn't say anything. I was busy thinking. If I wore a sombrero and mismatched shoes at school tomorrow, no one would ever want to be my friend.

As we got to our little house, I heard loud thumping noises coming from across the street. Ajay stood in his driveway, dribbling a basketball. He launched a shot that didn't even hit the backboard. Then he caught the ball, held it under one arm and waved at me.

I glared at him with a gigantic frowny face.

Ajay only wanted to be my friend when there were no boys around.

This was definitely my second-worst day ever.

FALLING FASHION FORWARD

The next morning Mum gave Lila and me giant red, green and white sombreros.

Lila put hers on. I could hardly see her face under the bright sombrero. She looked very silly.

"Are you sure today is Crazy Hat Day?" Lila asked me.

"Positive," I said.

"But I never forget anything. I don't remember my teacher saying anything about hats," she said. "How could I forget it's Crazy Hat Day?"

"I think your brain has been slowly oozing out of your head," I said. "I saw some grey matter on your pillow this morning."

Lila frowned. She took off the sombrero and rubbed the top of her head.

I laughed.

"It's not funny," Lila said.

You can't stop someone from laughing by saying something isn't funny. In fact, saying something isn't funny usually makes people laugh even harder.

Lila pointed to my feet. "Is it Crazy Shoe Day too?"

"Mismatched shoes are the latest style in France," I said.

"They look like the *lamest* style," Lila said as she put on the huge sombrero again.

Mum put the other sombrero on my head and took pictures of Lila and me. Then she said, "You girls can walk to the bus stop by yourselves."

Once we left the house, Ajay called from across the street, *"Buenos dias!* Is there a fiesta I don't know about?"

"Crazy Hat Day, right?" Lila called back.

"The school doesn't do that until May," Ajay said.

"Shelby, you tried to trick me!" Lila said. She threw her sombrero on the porch.

I shook my head and tossed my sombrero on top of Lila's. I said, "It was just a mistake."

Lila rolled her eyes.

On the bus, I had a seat to myself again.

Once I got to school, I saw my new friend Tessa outside our classroom. She wore a high-heeled boot on one foot and a flat sandal on the other. She was limping very slowly towards our classroom and muttering, "Ow, ow, ow." She looked as silly as my sister had looked in the giant sombrero.

"You look fashion forward," I told Tessa.

She turned around. "Thank you. I love fash – oof!" Her foot slipped in its high-heeled boot, making Tessa tumble over. Her sandal flew off on the way down and came to rest on the floor beside her.

I hurried to her and helped her up.

Brooke came by and said, "Tessa, you're so clumsy."

"It's hard to walk in mismatched shoes," Tessa said as she put her sandal back on. "I've already fallen over three times this morning."

"Being fashion forward is worth it," Brooke said. "I'm wearing a high-heeled sandal and a ballet slipper. I can walk perfectly – ow!" She tottered on her high-heeled sandal before falling straight to the floor and landing on her bottom.

Tessa and I helped her up.

"You know what?" Brooke said with a grimace. "I just heard mismatched shoes are going out of style. We will wear matching shoes from now on."

"Hooray!" Tessa jumped with joy.

On the way down, she fell to the floor again.

Brooke and I helped Tessa get up. Then the three of us walked into the classroom arm in arm. I was so glad to have friends to sit with in class.

But Ms Fish spent the first few minutes of class assigning everyone seats. Brooke, Tessa and I had to sit at different tables. Even worse, I was assigned to the same table as Ajay.

10

UNLUCKY AT LUNCH

As I sat at my new table, I turned away from Ajay. I said hello to the other boy there, a short kid who wore a grey T-shirt and a scowl. **Then I held up a ruler, bowed my head, and said, "Your majesty. King of the classroom."**

I heard Ajay laugh. I ignored him.

The boy next to me kept scowling and said, "I don't get it."

"It's a ruler," I explained. "Someone who rules. King of the classroom."

The boy shrugged. Ajay kept laughing. And I kept ignoring him.

"Today we will learn all about the maths you'll be doing this year," Ms Fish said.

"Great!" I whispered. "After we learn all about it today, we won't have to learn any more maths until next year."

Ajay laughed harder.

The boy next to me said, "Really?"

"I was joking," I said.

The boy shrugged again. "I don't get it."

"Settle down, everyone," Ms Fish said.

"Do you know what our teacher's favourite vegetable is?" I whispered.

"Quiet peas," Ajay said.

The other boy finally laughed. I glared at Ajay.
He had blabbed the punch line to my joke.

The rest of my morning went like this:

Maths lesson for about a thousand hours.

Break time for about two seconds.

Read a thousand-page chapter in our history textbook.

Finally, it was lunchtime. I sat with Brooke and Tessa again.

I smiled at them. "How's it going?"

Brooke took a big, angry bite of her apple. "I have a bad bruise from falling down this morning."

"Me too," Tessa said. "I love fashion. But my feet are killing me."

"A five-year-old girl came over and talked to me at break," Brooke said.

"How sweet!" I said.

"She pointed to my shoes and asked if I was a clown. When I told her I wasn't, she said my mummy should help me match my shoes." Brooke spat out an apple pip.

"That little girl isn't fashion forward," I said.

Brooke glared at me. A large piece of red apple peel was stuck between her front teeth. "I don't believe wearing mismatched shoes is a French fashion," she said. "In fact, I don't believe it's a fashion anywhere."

"Did you really live in France?" Tessa asked.

I nodded and said, "*Oui, oui*."

"My baby sister says *wee wee* when she has to use the potty," Tessa said.

I laughed.

Tessa and Brooke glared at me.

"*Oui, oui* means *yes, yes* in French," I said. I had looked it up on the internet last night.

"Did you look that up last night?" Brooke asked.

"No, no," I said. "That means *no, no* in French."

"I know," Brooke said.

"But do you know, know? That means you doubly know in English," I joked.

Tessa laughed.

Brooke frowned at her.

Tessa stopped laughing.

"I also looked up French words last night," Brooke said. "How do you say *T-shirt* in French?"

I gulped. "That's a hard one."

Brooke crossed her arms. "It's *T-shirt*."

"It is?" I asked. Then I said, "I mean, right, it is."

"How do you say *dress* in French?" Brooke asked.

"Dress?" I guessed.

"No," Brooke said. "It's *robe*."

"That makes no sense," I said. "Then what's the word for *robe*?"

Brooke rolled her eyes. "How would I know? You're the one who said you speak French."

"Oh. Right."

"Oh. Wrong," Brooke said. "Find somewhere else to sit during lunch. We've had enough of your lies."

"Yeah," Tessa said. "You're not even fashion forward."

"You're fashion backward," Brooke said.

Tessa laughed harder at that joke than she had ever laughed at my jokes.

I slowly and sadly packed up my lunch bag. Then I looked for other kids to sit with.

Gabby sat alone, reading a book and twirling a strand of her long black hair. I didn't want to bother her.

Three boys who looked a little younger than me were sitting at a table and laughing. Maybe they liked jokes as much as I did.

"Can I sit here?" I asked.

One of the boys burped loudly. The other boys laughed.

I hoped the burp meant "yes".

I sat down.

Another boy burped even louder. The boys laughed again.

Then they tried to see how many burps they could do in a row. Each boy tried his hardest to burp without stopping.

They laughed the whole time.

I liked funny stuff, but this wasn't funny to me. It was kind of gross. I left the lunch table and wondered if I'd ever make a friend here.

IT'S RUFF OUT THERE

As soon as I got home from school, I hurried to my bedroom and threw my backpack on the floor.

Lila came into the room, took her books out of her backpack one by one, and carefully stacked them in a neat pile. Then she said, "I have a prickly problem."

My pretty, popular, perfect sister possessed a prickly problem? "What's wrong?" I asked eagerly.

"Two of my new friends are having birthday parties at the same time on Saturday. I don't know which party to go to." She let out a long sigh. "Life is so hard."

I rolled my eyes, walked out of the bedroom and closed the door behind me.

In the hall, a little boy with big brown eyes and dark brown hair rushed over and crouched behind me. He shuffled along close behind me as I walked down the hall.

I saw Mum standing at the other end of the hall. I said, "Do you know there's a small stranger in our house?"

"He's small, but he's not a stranger," Mum said. "He's Coop's new friend from preschool."

I was the only kid in this house with no friends.

"Don't let Coop find me!" the boy whispered. "We're playing hide-and-seek."

Coop ran out of his bedroom, straight towards me. He crashed into me and shouted, "Found you!"

I returned to my room for some peace and quiet.

That didn't work. Lila was blaring Dalton Dash's awful music and hanging up a huge poster of him.

"You're ruining my bedroom!" I said.

"*Our* bedroom," Lila said as Dalton Dash sang, "Kiss me, kiss me, baby, baby, baby." Then she kissed Dalton's poster, right on his paper lips.

Eww! I hurried out of the room.

Coop and his friend were playing a game involving a lot of running and screaming. They sounded almost as annoying as Dalton Dash.

I had to get out of the house.

"Mum!" I shouted over the boys' screams. "Can I take Mugsy for a walk?"

"After you pose for a few pictures for my blog," she shouted back. "I want to show off our new house."

"A few pictures" meant about a thousand pictures. Finally, after my mouth ached from all its fake smiling, I left the house with Mugsy.

I said, "Mugsy, neither of us has any friends here. We can be each other's best and only friends."

Mugsy lifted his leg and weed on our front porch. I hoped that meant he wanted to be my best and only friend. Then Mugsy barked excitedly and pulled on his lead.

A woman and her poodle walked towards us. That dog also barked excitedly and pulled on its lead.

The woman stopped and said, "Hello, Mugsy!"

"How do you know my dog's name?" I asked.

Mugsy and the other dog wagged their tails and sniffed each other's bottoms.

"I met your mother when she took Mugsy for a walk yesterday," the woman said with a bright smile. "Mugsy and my dog, Foofy, became friends. Your mother and I did too."

Great. Even my mum and my dog had made friends.

I kicked the pavement. Ow! I stubbed my toe.

I walked Mugsy for a while longer before

heading back home. When I went past Ajay's house, I was glad to see he wasn't outside playing basketball.

Then Ajay came outside and wheeled a large rubbish bin to the kerb. "Hi, Shelby," he said.

I ignored him and kept walking.

Mugsy stopped, crouched down and pooed on Ajay's lawn.

It was a huge poo. Yuck!

I bent down and put it in a plastic bag. Ajay laughed. I did not look at him.

"Make sure you pick up all the donkey poo," Ajay said.

I looked up. "What donkey poo?"

"That dog is the size of a donkey," he said.

A woman came out of Ajay's house. She walked over to me and held out her hand to shake. "I'm Ms Patel, Ajay's mother."

"Nice to meet you," I said. "I'm Shelby Bloom."

As we shook hands, Ms Patel said, "Welcome to the neighbourhood, Shelby. Ajay said you're nice and funny."

"He did?" I asked.

"I meant funny looking," Ajay joked.

"No, you didn't," his mother said.

Ajay blushed, his cheeks turning rosy.

"Ajay, you should take Honey Sue for a walk," his mother said. She looked at me and added, "Honey Sue is our dog. Ajay named her himself."

I giggled.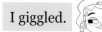

"I named her that when I was really little," Ajay said.

"We just got Honey Sue six months ago," Ms Patel said.

Ajay's cheeks turned dark pink.

"Be careful, Ajay," his mother said. "Last time you went for a walk, you stepped in dog poo. You got so upset."

Ajay's cheeks turned bright red.

I laughed.

Then Ajay laughed too.

Ajay's mum brought out Honey Sue. She was tiny and

fluffy. She barked at Mugsy, who whimpered and tried to hide his giant body behind my small one.

"Your dog is furry, but my dog is fur-ocious," Ajay said.

We laughed again.

"I saw you eating lunch with Brooke today," Ajay said. "Watch out for her. She can be mean."

"*Now* you tell me," I said. "My dog tried to warn me about Brooke too."

"He did?" Ajay asked.

I nodded. "Mugsy said Brooke was arf, arf, arful."

We laughed again.

Just then Dad shouted my name from our front porch.

"What?" I yelled back.

He started singing loudly: "Time for dinner! It's a winner! Chicken liver! So come in here!"

Now I was blushing. "My dad can be so embarrassing."

"Are you really eating chicken liver for dinner?" Ajay asked.

I shook my head. "It's just the only food that sort of rhymes with *dinner*."

"Too bad *cake* or *ice cream* doesn't rhyme with *dinner*," Ajay said.

"I'd better go before my dad starts singing again," I said. Then I gave Ajay a friendly wave goodbye and returned home wearing a big grin.

HOLD YOUR HORSES

At lunchtime the next day, two girls from my class waved at me. I sat next to them, hoping they would be my friends. Gabby sat nearby, reading a book.

One of the girls asked me, "Do you like Dalton Dash as much as we do?"

I shrugged. "That depends. If you can't stand him, then I like him as much as you do."

Gabby looked up from her book and laughed.

"Huh?" the girl asked.

"We love Dalton Dash!" her friend said.

Then they started singing, "Ooh, ooh, ooh! Love and kisses! Ooh, ooh, ooh! A dove and wishes!"

I made up my own words. "Ooh, ooh, ooh! I can't listen!"

Then I got up and looked for another place to sit.

"Shelby!" a blonde girl called out. "Do you want to sit with us?"

I smiled and sat next to her.

A red-haired, freckled girl across the table said, "Hi, Shelby."

"We know you're Shelby because you're the only new kid in our year," the blonde girl said. "I'm Alice Nolan."

"I'm Rose Kowalski," the red-haired girl said.

"Nice to meet you," I said.

"Do you like horses?" Alice asked.

I nodded. I was scared of horses, but I wanted to fit in.

"We don't like horses," Alice said.

I sighed with relief. "To be honest, I am not a fan of horses."

Then Alice said, "We don't like horses. We *love* horses."

Rose frowned. "Shelby, you're not a fan? Why not?"

"I'm not a fan. I'm a *super* fan," I said.

"Horses are so pretty," Alice said.

"And so clever," Rose added.

"And so stable," I said. I was joking, but no one laughed. **"Stable. Get it?" I asked.**

Rose laughed politely.

"Hey, Shelby," Alice said.

"Hay is for horses," I said.

No one laughed.

"Do you want to hang out with us on Saturday?" Alice asked.

"Are you hanging out on Mane Street?" I asked.

No one laughed.

"Get it? Mane Street. M-A-N-E instead of M-A-I-N."

Alice laughed politely.

I gave up. "I'd love to hang out with you guys," I said.

"Great," Alice said. "Meet us at Gold Star Stables at ten o'clock."

"Make sure you wear trousers," Rose said. "We're going horse riding!"

"Horse riding?" I gulped. "Like riding on the back of horses?"

"We don't ride on the front of horses." Rose laughed. "You're so funny, Shelby!"

That time I hadn't meant to be funny.

"I heard the horses at Gold Star Stables are very fast and very big," Rose said.

"Do you think I could get a very slow, very small horse?" I asked. "Maybe a really tired pony?"

Rose laughed again.

I hadn't meant to be funny that time either. It's hard to be funny when you're terrified.

I needed to find a way to get out of horse riding.

A LONG FACE AFTER A LONG DAY

By dinnertime I had a plan to get out of horse riding. Rose and Alice seemed very nice, but horse riding seemed very terrifying.

As I ate my dinner, I said, "Mum and Dad?"

"Don't talk with your mouth full," Lila said.

I turned to Lila, pushed food to the tip of my tongue and opened my mouth wide.

"Yuck!" Lila said.

"Shelby, behave," Mum said.

"Lila interrupted me," I said. "I was trying to ask you if horse riding can be dangerous."

Dad nodded.

"People fall off horses and break half the bones in their bodies," Mum said.

That was just the answer I was hoping for.

"I've been invited to go horse riding on Saturday," I said. "But I'm sure you won't let me. It's too dangerous."

"You should be OK if you don't try to gallop or jump your first time," Dad said.

"You can go as long as you wear a helmet," Mum said.

"But you said I could break half the bones in my body!" I replied.

"Look on the bright side," Lila said. "If you break half your bones, the other half will still be unbroken."

I shook my head. "The bright side would be being in the hospital so I wouldn't have to share a bedroom with you."

After dinner my family went to the library. This library was a lot bigger than the one back in Bunktown, Ohio. I thought I could find anything I needed.

As I was walking in, Gabby was leaving. I wasn't surprised to see her. She was always reading at school. Tonight she carried a backpack that seemed heavier than she was.

"Did you check out every book in the children's section of the library?" I joked.

"Just a large collection of boulders," she joked.

I laughed. Then I said, "I thought this library would be a lot taller. I heard it had thousands of storeys."

Gabby laughed.

When I got inside, I headed to the online catalogue and looked up joke books. There were a lot at this library!

I hurried to the jokes section. Most of the shelf was empty. The best joke books were gone.

I went over to the section with horse books.

Dad followed me. He asked, "Why the long face?"

"I get the joke. Horses have long faces," I said. "That's an old one."

"I wasn't joking. I was asking why you seem so sad," Dad said.

"Oh," I said. "Someone borrowed all the good joke books from the library. I have to settle for horse books."

Dad picked one up and leafed through it. "Do you know which side of a horse has more hair?"

"The outside," I said. "That's an old joke too."

Still, I couldn't help laughing. I checked out one book on grooming horses and another about breeds of horses. I wished the library had books on how to keep from falling off a horse and breaking half the bones in your body.

"You must be excited about going horse riding," Dad said.

I nodded. If *excited* meant *terrified*, then I was very excited.

A PEST FOR A PEST

When Lila and I arrived at the bus stop the next morning, Lola exclaimed, "Hooray! Lila's here!"

"I'm here too," I said.

Lola shrugged.

"Hey," I said loudly. "What's the difference between a bus driver and cold medicine?"

"What?" Ajay asked.

"A bus driver knows the stops. Cold medicine stops the nose," I said.

Ajay and a couple of other kids laughed. But when we got on the bus, Ajay sat in front of me with another boy. No one sat next to me.

I tapped Ajay on the shoulder and said, "Do you want to take our dogs for a walk together after school today?"

The boy next to Ajay said, "It's not cool to be friends with a girl."

"Shelby is funny," Ajay said. "But she's just my neighbour. We're not exactly friends."

I glared at him.

"You boys are mean," Lila said from across the aisle. "Shelby hasn't made a single friend here. You should be her friend."

Lila made me seem so pathetic. I said, "I've made two friends here. On Saturday we're going horse riding together."

"So you can break half your bones in your body," Lila said.

"Yes," I said. "I mean, yes about horse riding. Not about bones breaking."

Making new friends wasn't worth breaking half the bones in my body. It might be worth breaking one small bone, like a bone in my little finger. But I wouldn't want to break something big, like my skull. Or my skull and half my other bones.

When class started, Ms Fish said, "Let's review some rules of grammar."

I said, "Double negatives are a big no-no."

Ajay and a few other kids laughed.

Brooke said, "Shelby, *you're* a big no-no."

"Girls, do not interrupt me," Ms Fish said. "You can talk at break time."

"I hope not," Brooke said.

A lot of kids laughed.

I couldn't believe it. Brooke had got more laughs than I had. She made me so mad!

Luckily, I had other friends now. At break time, I hung out with Alice and Rose. They were drawing pictures of horses.

"I hope we get to ride fast horses on Saturday," Rose said.

"I want to go like the wind!" Alice said.

"I want to go like a jaguar," Rose said.

"I want to go back to class," I said.

I did. The classroom was empty. I reached into my backpack and headed for Brooke's table.

The bell rang a minute later. Kids started walking into the classroom.

I watched Brooke as she went to her desk and pulled out her chair.

"Ack!" she screamed.

"What's wrong?" I asked.

"Huge! Giant! Awful! Insect!" she screamed.

I walked over, reached down and plucked the huge, giant, awful insect from Brooke's chair.

"It's just a toy," I said.

The class laughed.

Brooke clenched her fists and yelled, "Who is the horrible person who did that?"

"Not me," "Not me," "Not me," the whole class said.

Well, the whole class except for me. I didn't say anything.

Gabby looked at me and winked.

I winked back at her.

I was grateful for my life motto: You never know when you'll need a large fake insect.

SATURDAY/ BONE-BREAKING DAY

On Saturday my mum drove me to Gold Star Stables. When we got there, I pretended to sneeze. Then I rubbed my eyes, pretended to sneeze again and made a wheezing sound.

"Oh no! I must be allergic to horses," I said. "We should go back home."

"We haven't even got out of the car yet." Mum

opened her door. "You're not allergic to huge, hairy Mugsy. You shouldn't be allergic to horses."

"Didn't you hear me sneeze?" I asked. "If I'm not allergic, I must be sick. I should go home and rest."

"Shelby's here!" Rose called out.

"Our new friend!" Alice exclaimed.

I didn't want to let down my new friends. I took a deep breath. Then I forced myself to get out of the car and join Rose and Alice.

"Howdy. I'm Cowgirl Keesha," a woman said. She wore a cute cowboy hat and boots. She walked towards us, leading a scary, gigantic brown horse with a thick white mane.

"Stranger danger!" I said. "We'd better go home right away!"

Mum and my friends laughed as if I were kidding.

As Cowgirl Keesha walked over and tied the horse to a post, Mum took a thousand pictures of Cowgirl Keesha's smiling face, the horse's scary face and my alarmed face.

"Sorry about my mum," I told my new friends. "She's taking pictures for her blog. She posts on it a thousand times a day. It's so embarrassing!"

"My blog is called Mum-O-Rama," Mum said proudly. "I have more than a hundred thousand followers."

"Wow!" Alice said. "You're really popular!"

"Will you take some pictures of us for your blog?" Rose asked.

"Shelby, your mum is pretty famous. You're so lucky," Alice said.

I didn't feel lucky. But I nodded and said, "My mum is cool." That was the first time I had ever used *mum* and *cool* in the same sentence.

Cowgirl Keesha pointed to a pile of helmets and told us to put one on.

"I don't think I should wear a borrowed helmet," I whispered to Mum. "I could get nits. And I can't ride a horse without a helmet. We'd better go home."

"You're so funny, Shelby," Mum said. "You'll be fine."

94

I sighed and put on the helmet.

Then Cowgirl Keesha pointed to three more scary, humongous horses. She said, "Come over here and groom the horses."

I slowly walked over. The three horses were tied to rails. One was gold, one was brown and one was black. They were beautiful. But they were also humongous and scary.

Alice and Rose followed behind me, walking even slower than I was.

Something funny was going on with them – and not funny in a *ha-ha* way. I turned towards Alice and Rose and asked, "How often do you do this?"

"We've never been here before," Rose said.

"We've never even been near horses before," Alice said. "We've only seen pictures of them."

"They look a lot bigger here than they do in pictures," Rose said.

"And scarier," Alice said.

The gold horse whinnied and stomped its big hoof.

"Yikes!" I said.

If all three of us broke half the bones in our bodies, that would be a lot of bones.

COWGIRL SHELBY

When I saw the horses up close, they seemed less scary. They had dark, dewy eyes and long legs and thick manes like shawls. They were bigger than Mugsy, but not as hairy. And they seemed a lot calmer.

Cowgirl Keesha took something out of a metal box and held it up. She said, "Do you know what this is?"

"A currycomb," I said.

"Right." She held up something else. "And what's this?"

"A hoof pick," I said.

"You must have a lot of experience with horses," Cowgirl Keesha said.

The truth was, I had about as much experience with horses as I did with French fashion. And lying about living in France had worked out terribly for me. I needed to tell the truth.

"I've never groomed a horse or ridden on one," I said. "I just read a couple of books about horses."

"It's a lot more fun being with horses than reading about them," Cowgirl Keesha said.

"It certainly is," I said.

Alice and Rose didn't say anything.

"Are you girls ready to brush the horses' coats and clean their hooves?" Cowgirl Keesha asked.

Rose shook her head.

"That sounds scary," Alice said.

"Ready!" I said.

I started brushing the gold horse.

"She's so soft and pretty! You should try it," I said.

Rose and Alice started brushing the other horses.

Cowboy Keesha helped us.

Mum shot a video of us.

The horses looked even more beautiful after we brushed and combed them and put spray on their coats to make them shine. I was the only one brave enough to lift the horses' legs – one at a time, of course – to clean their hooves.

"This isn't scary at all," Alice said.

"It's fun," Rose said.

Saddling the horses was hard work. First we had to put a thick pad on the horse's back. Then we had to hoist a saddle, which weighed about a thousand pounds, over the horse. Then we had to tie a lot of things on the saddle and connect it to the bridle and make sure the stirrups were the right size.

Cowgirl Keesha helped us. Honestly, she did most of the saddling.

"Drawing pictures of horses is a lot easier than saddling them," Rose said.

"It gets easier with practice," Cowgirl Keesha said. She saddled her gigantic horse in about two seconds.

"Can I ride the smallest, slowest one?" Alice asked.

"I thought you wanted to ride a racehorse," I said.

Alice shook her head. "I would like a baby pony who hasn't learned how to run yet."

"I'm scared," Rose said. "I don't even want to ride a baby pony."

"I thought you loved horses," Alice said.

Rose shook her head. "I only said that because I liked you and I wanted to be your friend."

"I'll still be your friend, even if you don't like horses," Alice said. "You don't have to get on a horse."

"But you should try it," I said. "You might like it."

"You're just saying that because you're a horse expert," Rose said.

"I also just pretended to like horses to be your friend," I admitted. "But now that I'm here, I love horses! If we all ride together and with Cowgirl Keesha, it won't be so scary."

"OK," Rose said.

"OK," Alice said.

"Yeehaw!" I said.

Cowgirl Keesha helped us get on the horses. Then she took us on a trail ride. The horses walked slowly in a line. I liked sitting high in the saddle. We saw a sparkling stream and leafy green trees and heard birds softly tweeting.

"Yeehaw! This is so much fun!" I said. "Can we go faster?"

"No!" Rose and Alice both said. They did not look like they were having fun. They looked like they wished they were anywhere except on the backs of their horses.

I couldn't think of anywhere I liked better. I was glad I had been brave enough to go to the stable. I was also

glad my mum hadn't taken me home when I'd asked her to.

I had tried a lot of things since school started. I had discovered I didn't love fashion like Brooke and Tessa. I didn't even like it much. I also didn't like listening to a thousand burps at lunchtime. I *definitely* did not like listening to Dalton Dash. But I loved horses.

After the trail ride, we gave our horses goodbye hugs.

"It was really fun horsing around with you," I said, "but it's time to rein it in."

Alice and Rose laughed.

I was happy they were my friends – even though they didn't love horses like I did.

STILL NOT CRAZY HAT DAY

On Monday I took the bus to school and sat by myself again. But this time I was reading a book about horses. You're never really alone when you have a good book.

When I got to school, I noticed Brooke and Tessa standing outside the building, wearing matching red hats that flopped to one side.

Brooke said, "These are berets from France. You probably don't even know what a beret is."

"Now I see what it is." I pointed to Brooke's beret. "A beret is a very silly looking hat."

"You just don't understand fashion," Brooke said.

"We love fashion," Tessa said.

"I may not understand fashion, but I know what's funny." I pointed to Brooke's hat again.

Brooke sneered. Then she said in a loud voice, "Listen up, everyone! Shelby Bloom never lived in Paris. She is the biggest liar in the world."

"You're exaggerating," I said. "There are probably a thousand billion bigger liars than me."

"Leave Shelby alone," Rose said, walking up with Alice.

"Yeah," Alice said. "Shelby's our friend."

Ajay came over too. "She's my friend too."

"Boys can't be friends with girls," a boy said.

"If they can't be friends, then how do you explain Shelby and me?" Ajay asked.

I smiled. "Not being friends with someone just because you're not exactly the same is like going around in circles. It's pointless."

"None of us are exactly the same," Ajay said.

"But since we're all standing outside, that means we're all outstanding," I said.

The kids laughed.

I was so lucky to have found friends here – real friends I didn't have to lie to.

I headed inside and saw Gabby sitting against a wall outside our classroom. She was reading a book as usual. Reading was fun, but I thought she'd like friends to talk to also.

I walked over to her and said, "What are you reading?"

She showed me the book cover. It was a library book called *A Thousand New Jokes for Kids*.

"Did you just check that out of the library?" I asked.

"Yeah. I took out lots of joke books," she said. "I love jokes."

"Me too," I said. "Do you want to sit with me and Rose and Alice at lunch today? We could share some jokes."

"OK," Gabby said. "I'll meet you in the place the young cows go for lunch."

"The calf-eteria," I said, and we both laughed.

D.L. Green has written **32** books for children and teens, including the Zeke Meeks and Silver Pony Ranch humorous chapter book series. Her books have been translated into six other languages. She lives in California, USA, and has a nice husband, three great kids and a spoiled dog. As well as writing funny books, she works as a lawyer.

Illustrator Leandra La Rosa lives and works in Palermo, Sicily. She was born in Trapani, a town on the island's western side, and since childhood her main interests have been illustration, animation and music. Leandra studied at the Academy of Fine Arts in Palermo and obtained a degree in graphic design. Since 2013 she has been working as a graphic designer and illustrator for many Italian agencies and publishing houses.

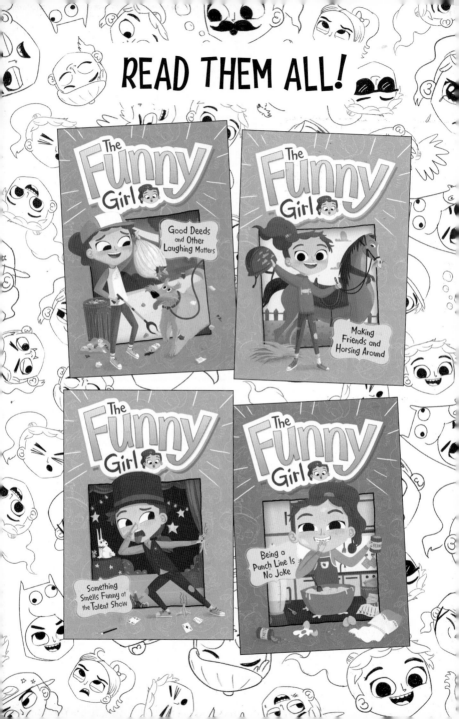